First American edition
Published by Henry Holt and Company, Inc.,
115 West 18th Street, New York, New York 10011.
Published simultaneously in Canada by Fitzhenry & Whiteside Ltd.,
91 Granton Drive, Richmond Hill, Ontario L4B 2N5.

Library of Congress Cataloging-in-Publication Data
Le Saux, Alain.
    [Papa roi. English]
    King daddy / by Alain Le Saux.
      (King daddy books)
    Translation of: Papa roi.
    Summary: While playing with his son, a father can be a doggy
daddy, cowboy daddy, or monster daddy.
    ISBN 0-8050-2193-0
    [1. Fathers and sons—Fiction. 2. Play—Fiction.] I. Title.
II. Series: Le Saux, Alain. King daddy books.
PZ7.L56243Ki   1992
[E]—dc20   91-44278

Printed in France
10 9 8 7 6 5 4 3 2 1

Imprimé en France
par Ouest Impressions Oberthur

king daddy

KING DADDY

BY ALAIN LE SAUX

HENRY HOLT AND COMPANY ▪ NEW YORK

doggy daddy

cowboy daddy

swing daddy

lion-tamer daddy

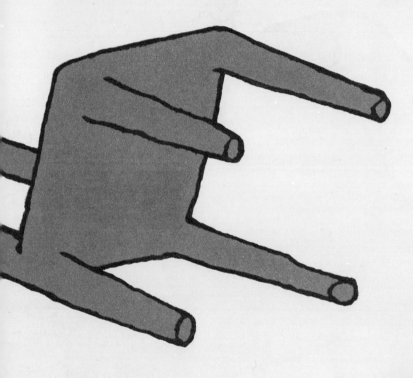

shadow daddy

pirate daddy

monster daddy

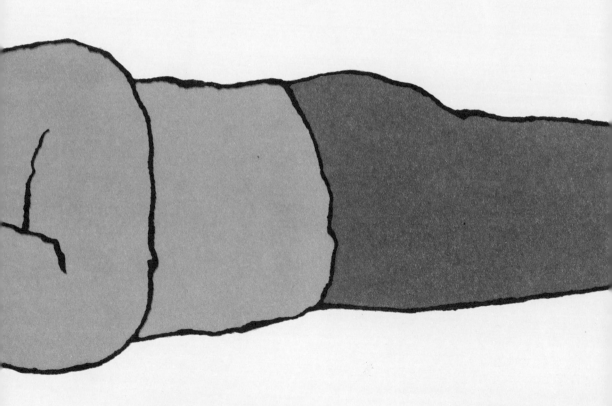

pony daddy

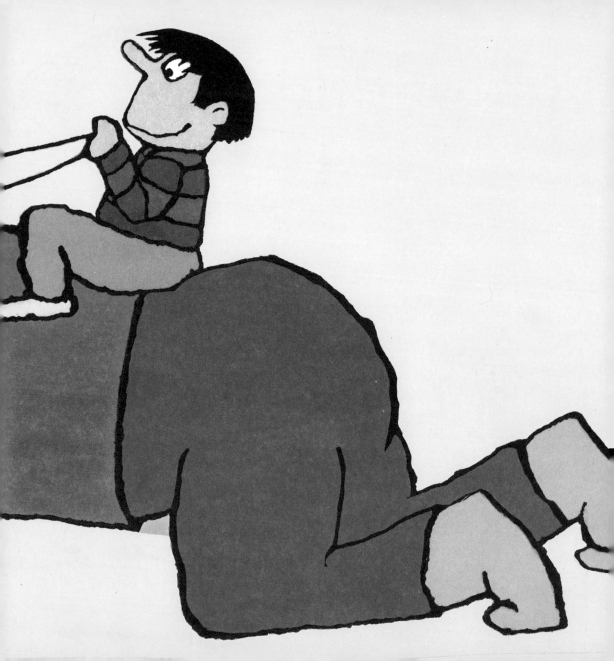

king daddy